Dark Man

The Dark Machine

by Peter Lancett

illustrated by Jan Pedroietta

Rans❀m

Chapter One:
Meeting in the Rain

The Old Man stands in a dirty doorway.

He is in the bad part of the city.

The wind howls and the rain lashes down.

It is day, but it is gloomy and the streets are empty.

The Old Man is waiting for the Dark Man.

Rain runs down his face, as he looks around.

He senses that someone is behind him and he turns.

The Dark Man is there.

"It is very clever, the way you move in the gloom without making a sound," the Old Man says.

The Dark Man grins, but the Old Man does not smile.

"Why are we meeting here so suddenly?" the Dark Man asks.

"Something dangerous has appeared in the city," the Old Man replies.

"It has been called here by the Shadow Masters, but they don't have it yet. You must see that they do not get it."

"If they called it here, why don't they have it?" the Dark Man asks.

"What they have called here is a Dark Machine.

"It is made of glass and stone and it is not very big.

"They used magic to call it from the Realm of Screams."

The Dark Man frowns.

Contact with the Realm of Screams is forbidden.

Once, he saw a man who had tried to make contact.

That man was insane and could never sleep.

He had to be strapped to his bed and fed through a tube.

"The machine was called to an empty warehouse in this part of the city," the Old Man says.

"We have had word of that."

He looks at the Dark Man.

"It has been found by a little boy."

Chapter Two:
Not an Angel

Later, the Dark Man stands beneath a street lamp. The lamp is not lit - it is too early.

The rain still beats down and the wind still howls.

The Dark Man is waiting for a girl.

The Old Man had said that this girl will help him.
She can find the little boy.

The Old Man had said that the Dark Machine could make areas of darkness fall, even during the brightest, sunlit day.

The Shadow Masters could use it to allow their foul demons to operate.

They would no longer have to wait for night.

Rain soaks the Dark Man.

He looks around, down the gloomy street.

Someone is coming. He can just see that it is a girl.

She walks towards him, slowly. Even in the wind and the rain, she wears only a T-shirt and jeans.

The Dark Man sees that he has met her before.

It is Angela, the girl who looks like an angel.

The Dark Man shudders. He remembers that Angela is not an angel.

"Why do we let the Old Man send us out in weather like this?" Angela asks.

She smiles, but her smile is never friendly.

"For me, it is a duty," the Dark Man says.

Angela shakes her head.

"Well, he has a hold on me too. But I don't see this as duty."

The Dark Man ignores her.

"There is a little boy we must find," he says.

Angela's eyes narrow and her smile gets wider.

"I'll find him," she says. "Let's get going."

Chapter Three:
The Little Boy

The Dark Man follows her down the street,
through the lashing rain.

He knows that he must keep an eye on her.

He remembers the screams from the last time
she helped him.

They walk deep into the bad part of the city.

Buildings are tall, but empty. The walls are crumbling.

Angela stops, and the Dark Man stands behind her.

Angela lifts her head and seems to sniff the air. She turns to her left.

"This way," she says.

Angela is fast.

Soon, they come to a building that is unused.
The doors are rotten and hang open.

They push past the doors.

This building had once been a children's play area. It is a large room.

It is light, because half of the roof has fallen in.

Standing inside the doorway, the Dark Man and Angela hear the sound of giggling.

It is a little boy.

They turn, and for a moment they see him. He is holding something that looks like a small box. The box shines as he turns it.

It is the Dark Machine.

The Dark Man looks at Angela.

Her eyes are narrow and she is licking her lips.

The Dark Man grabs her arm.

The little boy giggles and holds the box in front of him.

Suddenly, it grows dark around him.

They cannot see him.

Angela gasps and steps back.

The Dark Man pulls a flat rock from his pocket.

He speaks magical words that the Old Man had told him.

Light flickers in the darkness.

Sometimes the little boy can be seen. He is scared.

Terrible screams come from the darkness.

The Dark Man turns to Angela, but she has gone.

Chapter Four:
The Demons

The Dark Man walks towards the darkness.

He sees shapes in the darkness when the light flickers.

They are twisted shapes. They reach for the boy and the box. They are demons from the Realm of Screams.

The Dark Man cannot go any closer. He knows that he will lose his mind.

He throws the magical rock into the darkness.

There is a blinding flash. The Dark Man is knocked back onto the ground.

When he rises, the large room is back to normal.

The boy and the box have gone.

The Dark Man knows that they have both been taken back to the Realm of Screams.

He feels sad because he was not able to save the boy. But at least the Dark Machine is gone.

The demons from the Realm of Screams cannot get through.

As he walks slowly through the wet streets, the Dark Man thinks he sees Angela.

She slips around a corner and is gone.

The streets will be dangerous tonight with her out there, he thinks.

But he cannot be everywhere.

And he is very tired.

The author

photograph: Rachel Ottewill

Peter Lancett is a writer, fiction editor and film maker, living and working in New Zealand and sometimes Los Angeles. He claims that one day he'll 'settle down and get a proper job'.